A Note to Parents and Caregivers:

Read-it! Readers are for children who are just starting on the amazing road to reading. These beautiful books support both the acquisition of reading skills and the love of books.

 The PURPLE LEVEL presents basic topics and objects using high frequency words and simple language patterns.

 The RED LEVEL presents familiar topics using common words and repeating sentence patterns.

 The BLUE LEVEL presents new ideas using a larger vocabulary and varied sentence structure.

 The YELLOW LEVEL presents more challenging ideas, a broad vocabulary, and wide variety in sentence structure.

 The GREEN LEVEL presents more complex ideas, an extended vocabulary range, and expanded language structures.

 The ORANGE LEVEL presents a wide range of ideas and concepts using challenging vocabulary and complex language structures.

When sharing a book with your child, read in short stretches, pausing often to talk about the pictures. Have your child turn the pages and point to the pictures and familiar words. And be sure to reread favorite stories or parts of stories.

There is no right or wrong way to share books with children. Find time to read with your child, and pass on the legacy of literacy.

Adria F. Klein, Ph.D.
Professor Emeritus
California State University
San Bernardino, California

Editor: Jill Kalz
Designer: Lori Bye
Page Production: Melissa Kes
Art Director: Nathan Gassman
Associate Managing Editor: Christianne Jones
The illustrations in this book were created digitally.

Picture Window Books
151 Good Counsel Drive
P.O. Box 669
Mankato, MN 56002-0669
877-845-8392
www.picturewindowbooks.com

Printed in the United States of America.

All books published by Picture Window Books
are manufactured with paper containing at least
10 percent post-consumer waste.

Library of Congress Cataloging-in-Publication Data
Labairon, Cassandra Sharri.
Harold Hickok had the hiccups / by Cassandra Labairon ; illustrated by
Justin Greathouse.
p. cm. — (Read-it! readers: tongue twisters)
ISBN 978-1-4048-4881-8 (library binding)
[1. Tongue twisters—Fiction. 2. Hiccups—Fiction.] I. Greathouse, Justin, 1981– ill.
II. Title.
PZ7.L1113Har 2008
[E]—dc22
2008006332

Harold Hickok Had the Hiccups

by **Cassandra Labairon**
illustrated by **Justin Greathouse**

Special thanks to our reading adviser:

Adria F. Klein, Ph.D.
Professor Emeritus, California State University
San Bernardino, California

PICTURE WINDOW BOOKS
Minneapolis, Minnesota

Hillary Hunn hiked the hills behind her home.
She hummed a happy *hmmm-hmmm-hmmm*.

One hot day, Hillary Hunn hiked over a field of
hay. She heard HICC-UP! HICC-UP! HICC-UP!

No hog or hound could make that silly sound.

Then Hillary saw Harold Hickok high on a hay bale. He said, "HICC-UP! HICC-UP! HICC-UP!"

Harold Hickok had the hiccups. The hiccups Harold Hickok had.

"Help!" hollered Harold. "Help me halt these hiccups, Hillary Hunn!"

"Hold your breath, Harold Hickok," Hillary said. "That should halt the hiccups."

"I tried, Hillary," Harold said. "It didn't help."

"Stand on your head," Hillary said.

Harold tried. But his hiccups didn't halt.

Harold Hickok had the hiccups. The hiccups
Harold Hickok had.

"Hop to stop the hiccups, Harold," Hillary said. "Hop, Harold Hickok. Hop like a hare."

Harold hopped in the hay. He hopped like a hare. But the hopping hardly helped.

Harold Hickok had the hiccups. The hiccups
Harold Hickok had.

"What if I holler?" Hillary asked. "Hey, hiccups, hey! Go away! Hey, hiccups, hey! Go away!"

"Hush, Hillary, hush!" Harold said. "HICC-UP! HICC-UP! HICC-UP! My head hurts from your hollering. And I still have the hiccups!"

Hillary Hunn had a hunch. She hid behind some hay. She hoped to scare Harold.

"I hear you, Hillary," Harold Hickok said. "You're hiding behind the hay! Stop hiding. Help me halt these hiccups!"

Harold Hickok had the hiccups. The hiccups Harold Hickok had.

"Have hope, Harold," Hillary said. "I have ideas to help you heal!"

Hillary and Harold hung out with horses. They held out their arms and hovered like hawks. They hoot-hoot-hooted like owls. They how-how-howled like wolves.

"HICC-UP! HICC-UP! HICC-UP!" Harold said.
"Hooey! This isn't helping."

Harold Hickok had the hiccups. The hiccups
Harold Hickok had.

"Harold," Hillary said, "let's do homework."

"Homework?" Harold said. "I would rather help with housework than do homework. HICC-UP! HICC-UP! HICC-UP!"

"Follow me," Hillary said.

Hillary held Harold's hand as they hurried to her house.

Hillary Hunn and Harold Hickok hung hats on hooks. They hauled clothes from hallway to hamper. They cleaned the whole house.

"Hillary," Harold said, "this housework is hardly helping. HICC-UP! HICC-UP! HICC-UP!"

Harold Hickok had the hiccups. The hiccups Harold Hickok had.

"Hey!" Hillary said. "Honey heals hiccups! My mom makes hotcakes with homemade honey."

Mrs. Hunn wanted to help Harold, too. She made heaps of hotcakes with homemade honey.

"These hotcakes are heaven!" Harold hollered without a hiccup.

"Harold, you're healed!" Hillary said.

"Hillary, you're a hero!" Harold cheered. "You helped halt my hiccups! Hooray! Hooray!"

Hillary and Harold hugged. Then they hiked the hills behind Hillary's home, humming happily.

Harold Hickok had no more hiccups.

More *Read-it!* Readers

Bright pictures and fun stories help you practice your reading skills. Look for more books at your level.

Alex and the Team Jersey
Alex and Toolie
Another Pet
Betty and Baxter's Batter Battle
The Big Pig
Bliss, Blueberries, and the Butterfly
Camden's Game
Cass the Monkey
Charlie's Tasks
Flora McQuack
Kyle's Recess

Lady Lulu Liked to Litter
Marconi the Wizard
Peppy, Patch, and the Bath
Pets on Vacation
The Princess and the Tower
Sausages!
Theodore the Millipede
The Three Princesses
Tromso the Troll
Willie the Whale
The Zoo Band

On the Web

FactHound offers a safe, fun way to find Web sites related to topics in this book. All of the sites on FactHound have been researched by our staff.

1. Visit *www.facthound.com*

2. Type in this special code:
   1404848819

3. Click on the FETCH IT button.

Your trusty FactHound will fetch the best sites for you!
A complete list of *Read-it!* Readers is available on our Web site:
www.picturewindowbooks.com